To my teacher,
Jack Gantos
—D.D.

For Charlie and Cora, the
best little pizza-eating, couch-
jumping adventurers I know.
I love you goobers.
—D.S.

*He Wrote the ♡Book!♡*

*He Drew the Book!*

*Super BFFS!*

*Boring Stuff*

*RAWR!*

PHILOMEL BOOKS
an imprint of Penguin Random House LLC
375 Hudson Street, New York, NY 10014

Text copyright © 2018 by Drew Daywalt.
Illustrations copyright © 2018 by David Spencer.
Penguin supports copyright. Copyright fuels creativity, encourages diverse voices, promotes
free speech, and creates a vibrant culture. Thank you for buying an authorized edition of this
book and for complying with copyright laws by not reproducing, scanning, or distributing any
part of it in any form without permission. You are supporting writers and allowing Penguin to
continue to publish books for every reader.

Philomel Books is a registered trademark of Penguin Random House LLC.

Library of Congress Cataloging-in-Publication Data
Names: Daywalt, Drew, author. | Spencer, David, 1981– illustrator.
Title: The epic adventures of Huggie and Stick / Drew Daywalt ; illustrated by David Spencer.
Description: New York, NY : Philomel Books, 2018.
Summary: When a grumpy stuffed bunny and a happy-go-lucky stick fall out of their boy's
backpack, they embark on an odyssey that takes them all around the world, experiencing one
crazy adventure after another.
Identifiers: LCCN 2017041680 | ISBN 9780399172762 (hardcover) | ISBN 9780698182417 (ebook)
Subjects: | CYAC: Adventure and adventurers—Fiction. | Twigs—Fiction. | Toys—Fiction. | Diaries—
Fiction.
Classification: LCC PZ7.D3388 Ep 2018 | DDC [E]—dc23
LC record available at https://lccn.loc.gov/2017041680
Manufactured in China by RR Donnelley Asia Printing Solutions Ltd.
ISBN 9780399172762
10 9 8 7 6 5 4 3 2 1

Edited by Michael Green. Design by Ellice M. Lee.
Text set in Tw Cen MT, Amadeo Std and Scrawl Lighthouse.
The art was done in pen and ink and Adobe Photoshop.

H uggie and Stick belonged to a little boy named Reese, and like many things that belong to little boys, they spent a good part of their time being lugged around in a backpack. That is, until the day an open zipper, a large bump on the sidewalk, and Reese's bicycle combined to create an accident. This is their story.

It isn't pretty.

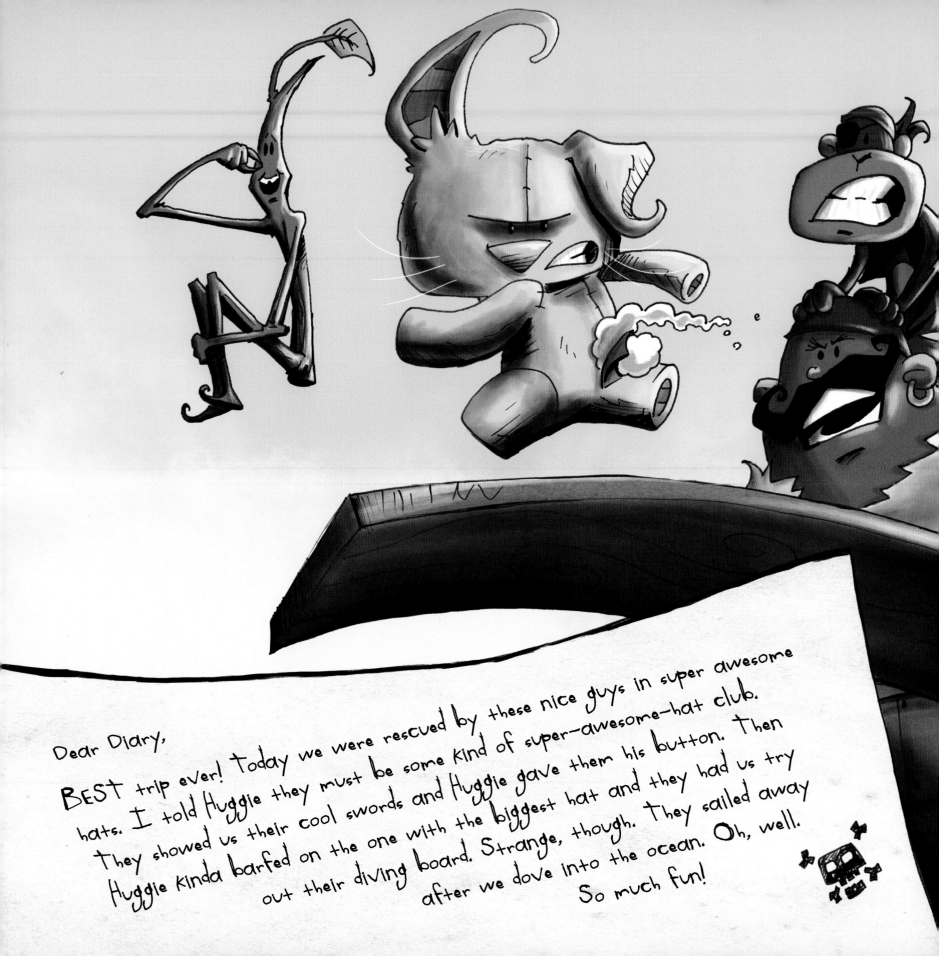

Dear Diary,

BEST trip ever! Today we were rescued by these nice guys in super awesome hats. I told Huggie they must be some kind of super-awesome-hat club. They showed us their cool swords and Huggie gave them his button. Then Huggie kinda barfed on the one with the biggest hat and they had us try out their diving board. Strange, though. They sailed away after we dove into the ocean. Oh, well.

So much fun!

WEDNESDAY—
Europe

Dear Diary,

I don't believe this. I almost get run over by a train and Stick gets knighted by the Queen of England?? In what universe is that fair? I'd chop him into little pieces with my new arm but it only seems to be good for eating hearty soups.

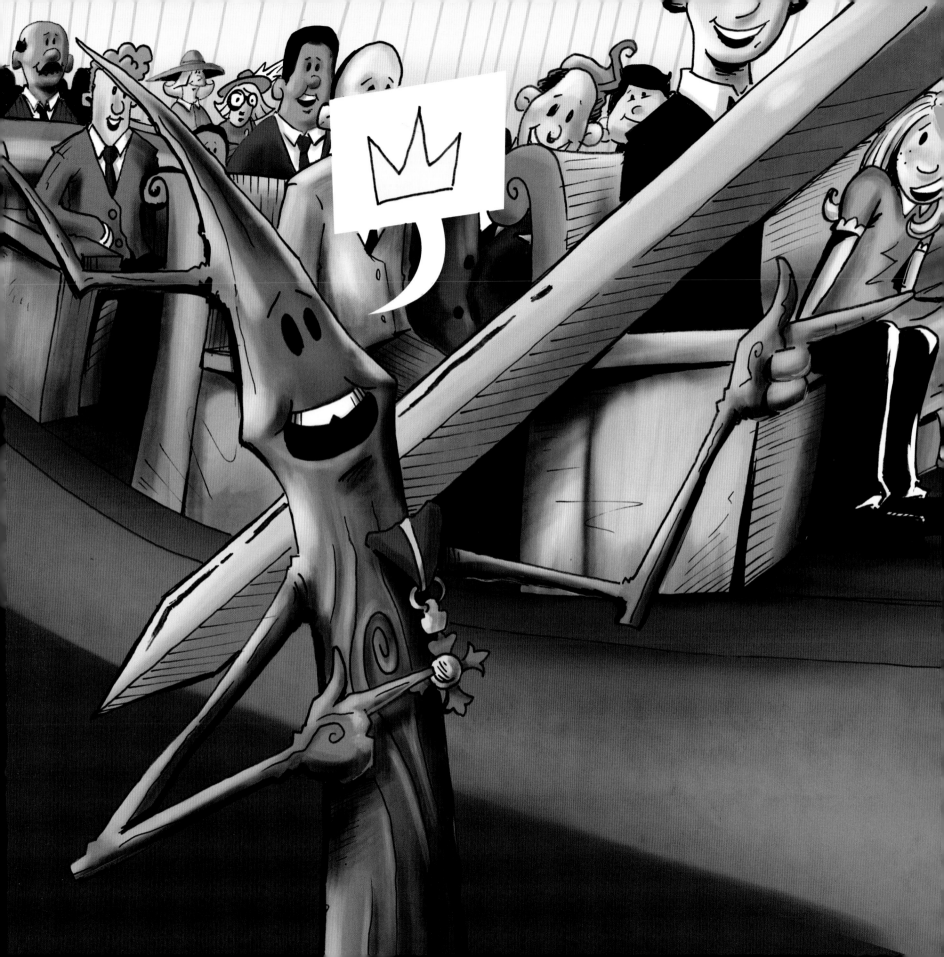

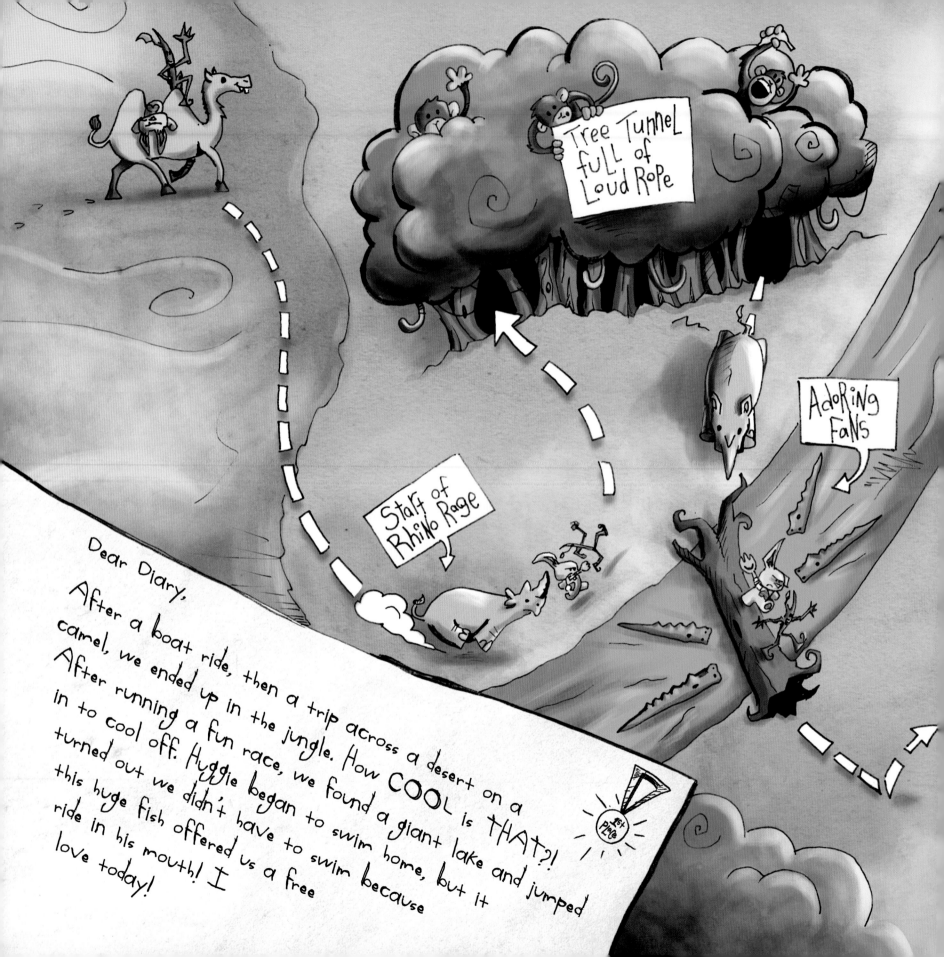

Tree Tunnel full of Loud Rope

Adoring Fans

Start of Rhino Rage

1st Place

Dear Diary,
After a boat ride, then a trip across a desert on a camel, we ended up in the jungle. How COOL is THAt?! After running a fun race, we found a giant lake and jumped in to cool off. Huggie began to swim home, but it turned out we didn't have to swim because this huge fish offered us a free ride in his mouth! I love today!

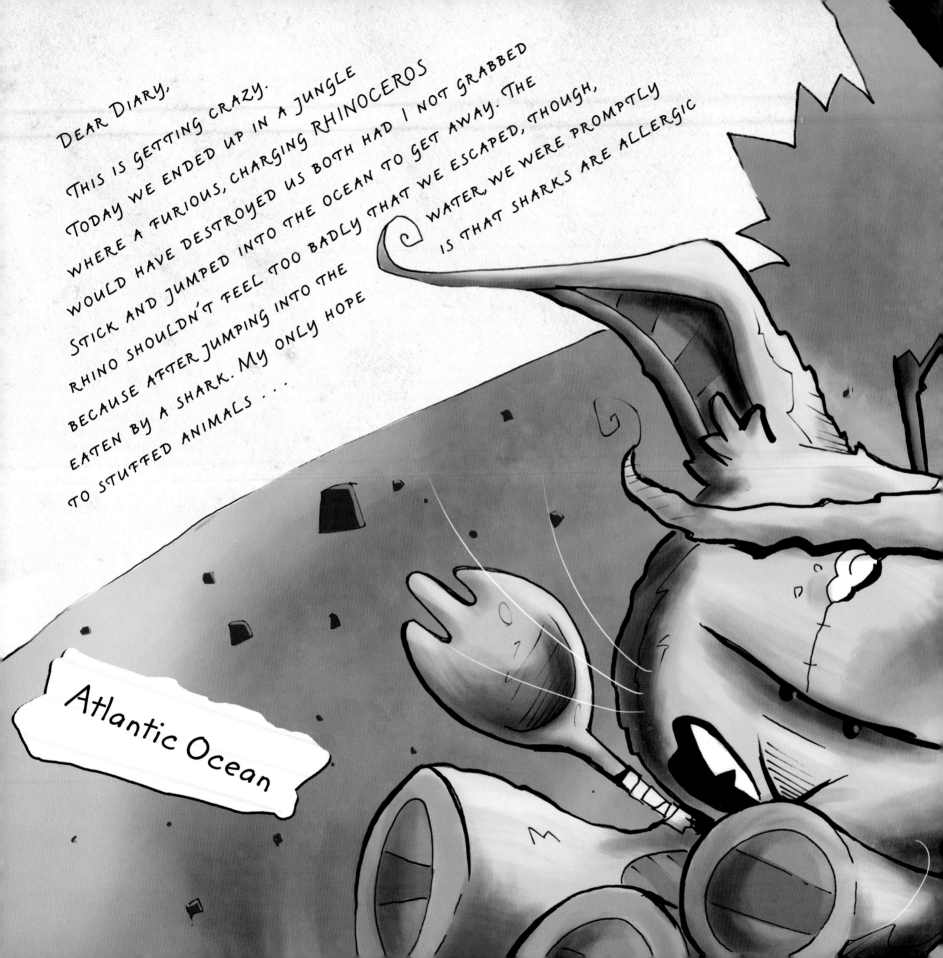

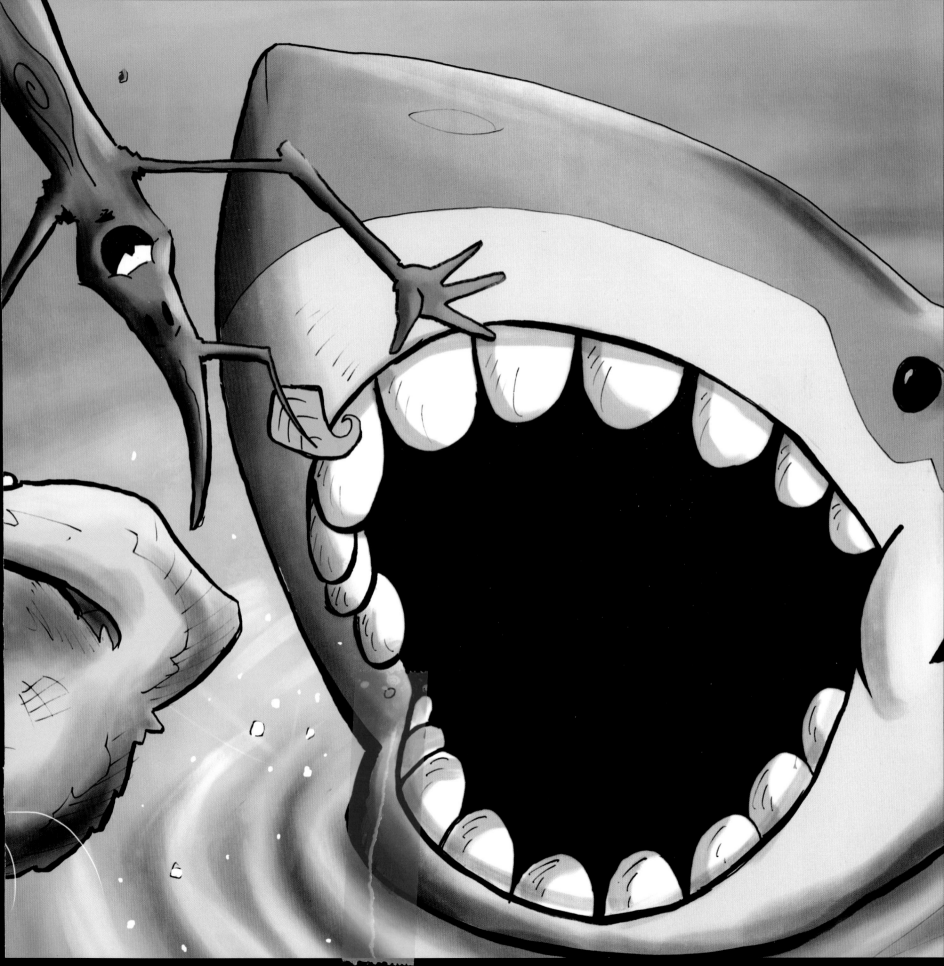

Dear Diary,

Holy moly!! Did you know sharks are allergic to stuffed animals? And he spit us up! SO COOL! Still enjoying our trip around the world, we swam to an ICEBERG! There were little elves in tuxedos living there! Sooo cuuuute! I wanted to eat them up! Unfortunately, they wanted to eat us too...

SATURDAY—
South America

NEW
Life Goals

Dear Diary,

Can you say "AmAZING!"? Because that's what the RAINFOREST is! All those cool animals. And those nice people who turned me into a sippy strawl!! I even saved Huggie from those mean fish that tried to eat him.

Golly gumdrops, Huggie and I make a GREAT team.

Dear Diary,

Stick slept through the llama ride, the train ride, two bus rides, the small plane trip, then 200 miles on the back of a very determined chihuahua. If I never go anywhere with that smiling piece of wood again, it will be too soon.

the next day . . .

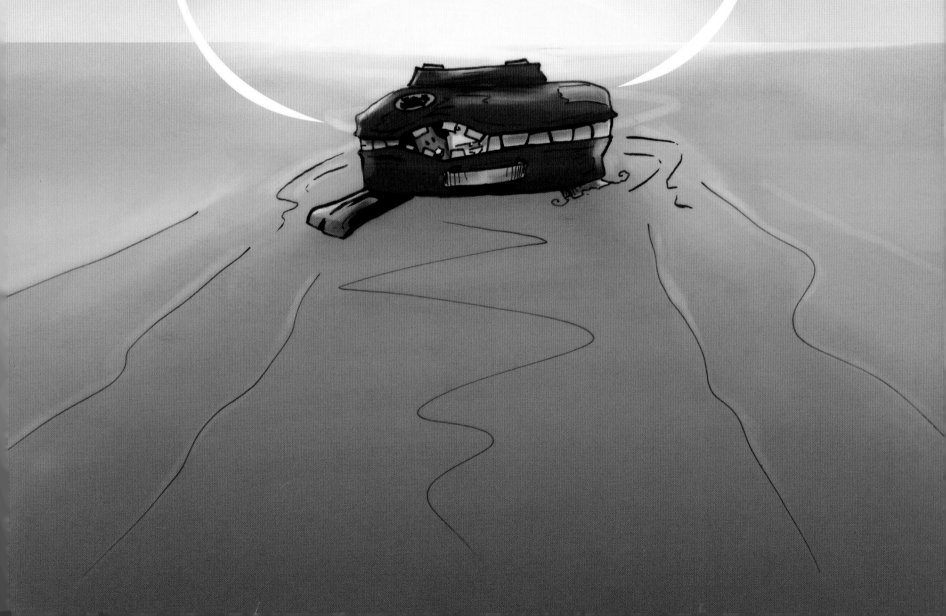

Arctic Ocean

ASIA

Europe

AFRICA

INDIAN OCEAN

AUSTRALIA

ANTARCTICA